Office Suite

Office Suite

Two one-act plays
by
ALAN BENNETT

FABER & FABER

London   Boston

First published in 1981
by Faber and Faber Limited
3 Queen Square London WC1N 3AU
Printed in Great Britain by
Lowe and Brydone Printers Limited Thetford Norfolk
All rights reserved

© *1981 by Alan Bennett*

British Library Cataloguing in Publication Data

Bennett, Alan
Office suite
I. Title
822'.914   PR6052.E5

ISBN 0–571–11744–9

INTRODUCTION

These plays were written for television. Since both take place in one-room settings they adapt naturally for the stage. I think. I am told there is a world of difference between writing for the theatre and for television, but what that difference is I have never fathomed. With television there is always the likelihood the audience is otherwise occupied; attention may have wandered, indeed the audience may have wandered, slipped into the scullery for a cup of something—a facility denied theatregoers, though, were it offered, the odds are they'd be up and out there in droves. At home television is just one of the things that may be going on; in the theatre there is only the play. The writer is supposed to take account of this difference, but how? One has to make television more riveting, I suppose. But then it all has to be more riveting, doesn't it? Ah well.

Both *Miss Prothero* and *Green Forms* are set in the north and are written in a northern idiom. Both are about northern women, or ladies rather, a class of person I find an unfailing delight. Bare words on the page cannot convey the rhythms of their speech or the nuances with which they invest it. Conversation is a conspiracy. When two women are talking in the street they do not look at one another but scan the horizon for possible eavesdroppers, the delivery of their explosive banalities subtly syncopated to take account of being overheard.

'He was four hours on the table. Five surgeons battled to save his life. He died three times. Finally Mr Cunliffe came out and asked me whether I wanted him resuscitating. . . . they live at Harrogate, his wife's a right refined woman, I've seen her having tea in Marshall and Snelgrove's. Anyway, I said "Well, Mr Cunliffe, if it's all the same to you, No." I didn't want him fetching backwards and forwards. Besides he wasn't like my husband, not at the finish.'

It is speech as mannered and dramatic as Restoration comedy and while it is a delight to listen to, it is not easy to perform.

People, by which I mean television producers, imagine northern speech simply as standard English with a dirty dishcloth accent, and northern women as southern women who can't speak properly.

They're not. Northern women are another species. They have come down by a separate genetic route and like the Galapagos turtles (whom some of them resemble) they have developed their own characteristics and attitudes. Hopes are doomed to be dashed, expectations not to be realized, because that's the way God, who certainly speaks with a southern accent, has arranged things. 'I'm not going to expect too much,' I heard a woman say once. 'The worst is the most I intend to expect, then I shan't be disappointed.'

This sense of foreboding is implicit in the structure of northern language. As with the Jews, grammar becomes an insurance taken out against disaster. Positive statements are made in a negative way. The north is the land of litotes.

'When you think he only has one arm he's not had a bad career. And she's not unpleasant. Of course, it's a goodish salary now, local government. I don't dislike this carpet.'

Northern ladies are accomplished storytellers, painting vivid pictures in a few dramatic strokes:

'Her hubby's on the critical list. He's in Intensive Care. They've got a daughter works for Johnson and Johnson. And they'd just got back from Barbados.'

And the Intensive Care is somehow a judgement for Barbados.

Key words will often come at the end of the sentence:

'It used to be a right refined place did Morecambe. I preferred it to Bispham. Only it's gone all hectic. I've watched it go hectic, Morecambe. And it'll go the same way will Grange. It's only a matter of time.'

Social distinctions are subtle and minute. There are advantages to be drawn from status, however lowly. Miss Prothero points out how her visits are much sought after:

'I've got half a dozen people who're always begging me to pop round, one of them a retired chiropodist.'

It's social climbing, albeit very much on the lower slopes. I was once on the top of a tram in Leeds with my aunty. We were passing Wellington Road gasworks. She laid a hand on my arm.

'That's the biggest gasworks in England,' she said. 'And I know the manager.'

Green Forms was first transmitted by London Weekend Television (under the title *Doris and Doreen*) on 16 December 1978 with the following cast:

DOREEN	Patricia Routledge
DORIS	Prunella Scales
MR LOMAX	Peter Postlethwaite

A Visit from Miss Prothero was first transmitted by the BBC on 11 January 1978 with the following cast:

MR DODSWORTH	Hugh Lloyd
MISS PROTHERO	Patricia Routledge

Both plays were directed by Stephen Frears.

Green Forms

DORIS RUTTER (MISS)
DOREEN BIDMEAD (MRS)
MR LOMAX
BOSWELL
MS DOROTHY BINNS

An office. Plants on the window ledge and postcards on the wall imply that though this is a place of work that is not the be-all and end-all. So the office is cosy if a little run-down: in one of the interior windows a pane of glass is broken; one lamp wants a shade, another a bulb; the Venetian blind lacks several slats and the rubber plant is plainly on its last legs. These dilapidations are precise and will turn out to be important.

In this office are three desks, one occupied by DOREEN, *a married lady in her thirties, another by* DORIS, *an unmarried lady in her forties; the third is empty and plainly unused.*

There are two doors, one to the corridor and the other to a passage at the far end of which is an unseen toilet and washbasin. The desks are furnished with the usual office clutter and there is an In/Out tray by the corridor door for incoming/outgoing mail. Shelves are lined with buff folders containing papers, some so fat they are tied up with string. Other folders are piled on chairs, in dusty brown paper parcels on the tops of tin office cupboards and some have accumulated on the floor round the desks. There is a mass of miscellaneous information here which a computer would put paid to in five minutes. However there is no computer, just DORIS, *who is reading the newspaper and* DOREEN, *who is contemplating her desk.*

DOREEN: Are green forms still going through Mrs Henstridge?
    (*Pause*)
DORIS: Newcastle.
DOREEN: Newcastle?
DORIS: Newcastle.
DOREEN: You don't mean Manchester, Fordyce Road?
DORIS: No. I mean Newcastle, Triad House.
DOREEN: Then where's Mrs Henstridge? (*Pause*) She was green forms for as long as I can remember. And now you say it's Newcastle. (*Pause*) *Newcastle?*
DORIS: Staff appointments and changes in personnel: Newcastle.
    (*The green form is inside an inter-office envelope. One look inside the envelope tells* DOREEN *the form is green and therefore not their pigeon. If she does take the form out of the envelope she should not read it.*)

DOREEN: Newcastle. Not Mrs Henstridge. Thin-faced woman. Blonde-ish. She had a son that wasn't right. Lived in Whingate.

DORIS: I don't know where people live.

DOREEN: Well where's she gone and got to if she's not doing green forms?

DORIS: Search me.

DOREEN: I can remember when it used to be Southport.

DORIS: It isn't Southport.

DOREEN: I'm not saying it is Southport. Southport is being wound down.

DORIS: Up.

DOREEN: Up what?

DORIS: Wound up.

DOREEN: Wound down. Wound up. Phrased out anyway. I hope she hasn't been made ... you know ...

DORIS: What?

DOREEN: Well ... redundant. I wouldn't like to think she's been made redundant; she was very nicely spoken.

DORIS: I haven't had the pleasure.

DOREEN: Mrs Henstridge? Oh yes. You'll have gone up in the lift with her many a time. Smartish, oldish woman. Check costume. Brown swagger coat.

(*Pause*)

Fancy them phrasing out Southport. I never thought they'd phrase Southport out.

(*Pause*)

DORIS: Phasing, not phrasing.

DOREEN: Come again?

DORIS: Phasing. The phrase is phase. Not phrase.

DOREEN: What did I say?

DORIS: Phrasing.

DOREEN: Oh. Well. If you'd come up to me ten years ago and said 'They're going to phase out Southport' I'd have laughed in your face.

DORIS: You wouldn't.

DOREEN: I would.

DORIS: You wouldn't. If someone had come up to you ten years ago and said 'They're phasing out Southport', you wouldn't have known what they were talking about: you didn't work here then.

(*Pause*)

DOREEN: How's Mother?

DORIS: Naught clever.

14

DOREEN: No. I didn't think so, somehow.

DORIS: Anyway, why single out Southport? I ran into Mr Butterfield in Planning and he says a question-mark definitely hangs over Ipswich.

DOREEN: Ipswich! That's only been going five years.

DORIS: Four. She was on the commode half the night again.

DOREEN: Poor lamb.

DORIS: I think she must have eaten something. You can't turn your back. Last time it was the vicar. I just caught him doling her out the Milk Tray, else that would have been another three o'clock in the morning do. She's on a knife edge. People don't realize. One coffee cream and it's three months devoted nursing down the drain. I'm trying to build her up.

DOREEN: What I'm wondering is . . . Where will the axe fall next?

DORIS: Axe? What axe? This isn't an axe. These are scheduled cut-backs. Selective redeployment as set out in the '78 report. Axe! I know one thing. It won't fall on yours truly.

DOREEN: Why not?

DORIS: Because I'm Grade 3, that's why.

DOREEN: Well I'm substantively Grade 3. Technically I'm Grade 4 but I'm holding down a Grade 3 job. If Central hadn't gone and frozen gradings I'd have been made up months since. Wouldn't I?

DORIS: They won't unfreeze gradings while differentials are depressed. Even in this cock-eyed group.

DOREEN: No. I know.

DORIS: I don't think people *are* out of work anyway. I was reading in the paper yesterday a firm in Warrington is sending £50,000 of seersucker slipovers to Finland. Does that sound like out of work?

DOREEN: I can't see myself in seersucker somehow. Even in Finland. Anyway I'm not going to worry: I've got Clifford.

DORIS: Oh, Clifford.

DOREEN: That's the thing about marriage, there's always the two of you.

DORIS: There's two of Mother and me.

DOREEN: We've talked it over and Cliff says that in the event of a real downturn in the economic climate he could fall back on the smallholding and me do my home hairdressing. People are always going to want their hair done, inflation or no inflation, and there's always a demand for rhubarb.

DORIS: Yes. Well. I hope it keeps fine for you.

DOREEN: 'Which twin has the Toni?'. Remember? It's stood me in good stead has that. You don't catch me in a salon. Only you think it's Newcastle? This green form.

15

DORIS: Newcastle.

DOREEN: (*As she addresses it and to herself*) Not . . . Mrs . . . Henstridge.
Off you go to Newcastle. (*She takes it to the Out tray by the door.*) We
are getting on this morning. Proper little beavers. Oh, the *Bulletin*'s
come. (*It is in the tray.*) You didn't tell me the *Bulletin* had come.
(*Reading from the* Bulletin.) 'It's goodbye to Leeds, Cardigan Road.
Smiles and sadness at simple ceremony.' Fancy shutting down
Cardigan Road. That would have been unthinkable five years ago. It
has its own canteen.

DORIS: What am I talking about? (*She goes over to the Out tray and takes
out the envelope with the green form.*) Doris Rutter, you want your
head examining. Newcastle?

DOREEN: Oh, little Brenda Horsfall's dead. 'Death will leave gap at
Goole.' You remember Brenda?

DORIS: Doreen.

DOREEN: You called.

DORIS: Smack me.

    (DOREEN *Smacks her outstretched hand without looking up from the*
Bulletin)
    This isn't Newcastle.

DOREEN: I never thought it was. I said all along it was Mrs Henstridge.

DORIS: It's not, though. That's what confused me, you introducing her.
Mrs Henstridge has got nothing to do with it.

DOREEN: Better smack me then.

    (DOREEN *gets smacked too.*)

DORIS: Under the new procedure this belongs on the second floor. It has
to go through Staff and Appointments.

DOREEN: Oh, nice Mr Titmuss.

DORIS: After that it goes to Newcastle. Hearken to the book of words.
    (DORIS *reads from a procedural manual.*) 'Selection and
Appointments, North Western Area. Newcastle, Triad House. PO
Box 230. Local and District Documentation:' (i.e. us) 'all
communications on a district level to be routed through Area Staff
and Selection with contingency copies to Records and relevant
departments concerned.' We're not a relevant department
concerned. Somebody on the second floor is living in the past.
Docket it 'misrouted' and bung it straight back to Staff Selection.

DOREEN: Mr Titmuss.

DORIS: The very same. No, let me. I want to append a note.

DOREEN: (*Still glued to the* Bulletin) 'Thirty-five years at Bristol, Hotwells
Road: veteran Reg. punches his last clock.'

16

DORIS: (*Typing*) 'Dear Stanley, don't I have troubles enough? What goes on down there on the second floor, or has your triumph in the badminton semi-finals gone to your head? Definitely your baby. Hard cheddar, Doris.' (*She staples it to the green form and puts it in the Out tray by the door.*) When were these pink forms due back in Personnel?

DOREEN: Last Monday.

DORIS: I suppose I ought to look through them. Though I don't see why we should break our backs for Mr Cunliffe. What have Personnel ever done for us? Except make our lives a misery.

DOREEN: (*Reading from the* Bulletin) 'Say Jack and Nanette. Any kindred spirit passing through Rugeley, Staffs., and wanting a natter about the old prehistoric days at Bebington Road, remember, folks, coffee time is from 9 a.m. to 11 p.m.' People are nice.

DORIS: Oh, Blood and Sand!

DOREEN: Language.

DORIS: That puts paid to Mr Cunliffe. No pink forms today. (*She holds up some forms.*) One PS104. Two PS104s. Three PS104s.

DOREEN: I don't believe it. What do they think we are?

DORIS: That's three hours' solid work. Three PS104s. I think a cigarette is called for.

(*The telephone rings.* DOREEN *answers it.*)

DOREEN: 3507 Precepts and Invoices, Mrs Bidmead speaking. One moment, Mr Cunliffe. I'll see if she's in.
(DORIS *shakes her head.*)
She appears to have slipped out. Can I be of any assistance? Well if we have any pink forms, and at this moment in time I'm not sure that we have, one thing I do know: we are not sitting on them. At a guess I should say they're somewhere in the pipeline. (*Putting her hand over the receiver.*) He's talking about shortfall.

DORIS: He wasn't talking about shortfall when Mr Parry had shingles.

DOREEN: You weren't talking about shortfall when Mr Parry had shingles. I seem to remember some of us working round the clock. (*Hand over the receiver.*) What does he tell the computer?

DORIS: That's his problem. He's been to Newport Pagnell.

DOREEN: Didn't they teach you that at Newport Pagnell? (*Hand over receiver.*) He says there's going to be an alteration. We'll be laughing on the other side of our faces. We won't know what's hit us. (*Shaken*) He's put the phone down. Doris.

DORIS: What?

DOREEN: What does he mean?

17

DORIS: It means he wants these pink forms. I was going to do them but I'm not now. People will just have to learn to be polite. Personnel. Let them wait. I can find something else to do. These 104s. No. I can't face them. If only we didn't have to bother with these silly, faffing forms we could get on with some real work.

(*She picks up the* Bulletin *which* DOREEN *has discarded.*)

DOREEN: Has it gone cold? It feels to me to have gone right cold.

DORIS: Something about Newport Pagnell here. 'Newport Pagnell comes of age. Smiling graduates of the twenty-first computer course at Roker Park gather round C.I.S.S.I.E. (Computer Instructor for Senior Staffs In Electronics).' Cissie! (*She reads the item scornfully.*) 'Cissie is now a rather battered old lady and is soon to be replaced by a more sophisticated model. By the time you read this the old girl will have done her last print-out. Sorry, Cis, but it happens to us all. Ed.'

DOREEN: I don't know why you don't go on a course or two.

DORIS: And where am I supposed to put Mother in the meantime?

DOREEN: Send her to that place at Bispham.

DORIS: I don't want to go on a course. You just want me out of the way.

DOREEN: It would improve your prospects.

DORIS: I don't want prospects. Prospects is what I don't want. Prospects means you get woken up in the middle of the night and asked to fly with Mr Swithinbank to Saudi Arabia. Why? Because you've got prospects and you've been on the Far East course. Though when you come in on a morning and find three PS104s on your desk maybe it's preferable.

DOREEN: What?

DORIS: Saudi Arabia. PS104, 104, 104. Office stinking precept forms. Who bothers with precept forms these days?

DOREEN: I hope she's not dead.

DORIS: Who?

DOREEN: Mrs Henstridge. I don't think she is. I seem to remember something about the Wirral.

DORIS: She's probably been sacked. What grade was she? Wasn't she your grade?

DOREEN: I don't know. Remind me to get Clifford some chops. He loves chops.

DORIS: When we say redundancy we mean you, Mrs Henstridge.

DOREEN: Tina's not on heat again, is she?

DORIS: No. Why?

DOREEN: You just seem a bit bitter today somehow.

18

DORIS: You'd be bitter if you'd got a shovelful of 104s on your desk. One for a lampshade. One, would you believe it, for an electric light bulb. And the other. (*She looks for it.*) Where is it? . . . Why don't they get stuff direct from Stores like everybody else. Precepting for individual items. A gross of light bulbs, yes. That's worth a 104. But *one*. It's procedurally correct, but it's insanity. If everybody started putting in a 104 whenever they wanted a light bulb we should be swamped. One of them is for a washbasin plug. When I can find it. *A washbasin* plug! Then people say you're looking older!

DOREEN: Listen. Tell me again. Mother. Which of her hips is the plastic one?

DORIS: It depends which way you look at her. Left if you're looking at her. Right if she's looking at you. Why?

DOREEN: It's just that Clifford's sister-in-law's had one fitted and I thought they might have a bit of something in common.

DORIS: Why? Which side is hers?

DOREEN: I don't know. I shall have to ask. Anyway, who says you're looking older?

DORIS: I do. Where is it?

DOREEN: What?

DORIS: This other 104.

DOREEN: What do you want it for?

DORIS: I don't want it. I just want to know where it is for when I do want it.

DOREEN: I wish I had your system.

DORIS: All this rigmarole. They cost 5p to buy. And just think what our time's costing.

DOREEN: We could apply for a washbasin plug if we wanted. We've lost ours.

DORIS: We haven't lost it. It was pinched.

DOREEN: It disappeared.

DORIS: Nicked. By Personnel.

DOREEN: Are you sure?

DORIS: Positive. What sort of a mentality is it pinches a plug from a washbasin? Several of them have degrees.

DOREEN: How do you know it was Personnel?

DORIS: I saw it.

DOREEN: Saw what?

DORIS: I saw our plug.

DOREEN: Where?

DORIS: In the toilet in Personnel.

DOREEN: On the fourth floor? What were you doing there?

19

DORIS: Looking for our plug.

DOREEN: How do you know it was ours?

DORIS: Because I recognized it.

DOREEN: They're standard issue.

DORIS: Listen. When it disappeared last time it was the third time in six months, so I thought 'Right, Doris. We'll settle these buggers.' So I got a new one and cut a little nick in it. Then a fortnight later it went again. Nicked.

DOREEN: You mean the one you'd nicked?

DORIS: I didn't nick it. I put a nick in it. The one I'd put a nick in was nicked. Right?

DOREEN: I see.

DORIS: Well, when they had everybody down in the canteen for the efficiency drive, I took the opportunity to do a little fact-finding survey of the departmental toilets.

DOREEN: Doris!

DORIS: And guess where Doris found it? Personnel.

DOREEN: Never.

DORIS: Positive. Little nick in it. It must have been. Nobody else in their right mind is going to put a nick in their washbasin plug, are they?

DOREEN: So why didn't you confront them with it? Lay it before Mr Skidmore.

DORIS: Do you remember Miss Batty of Costing?

DOREEN: Shy woman, a bit on the grey side. Wore a little blue coatee.

DORIS: Well she'd keep missing their toilet seat: she'd go down to Stores to put in for a replacement, it'd last about a fortnight then it would get pinched. She'd put in for another. Same thing. It got so that she daren't go into Stores.

DOREEN: I can imagine. She was a very refined woman.

DORIS: Eventually when she got to her sixth replacement Miss Batty got a red hot poker and burnt her name on the underside. Unfortunately they had somebody down from the sixth floor to do with industrial psychology. He was in Costing talking about incentives and said could he use the toilet? Well, I suppose, being from the sixth floor he lifted the seat and the upshot was Miss Batty got sent on three months' unpaid leave and lost her grading. Hypertension. She now looks after her brother in Rhyl.

DOREEN: Tragic.

DORIS: So don't ask me why I didn't take it up with Mr Skidmore.Only I know. And Personnel know I know.

DOREEN: Yes. We still haven't got a washbasin plug, though, have we?

20

DORIS: No problem. When I want to fill the basin, like when I do my foot, I use one of the issue paperweights. What do you want a plug for?

DOREEN: Same reason you want a rubber plant.

DORIS: What rubber plant?

DOREEN: I've got one now. A PS104. For a rubber plant.

DORIS: A PS104 for a rubber plant. Who puts in a PS104 for a rubber plant? (*Pause, as* DORIS *compares documents.*) The same person who puts in a PS104 for a washbasin plug. What's the personnel number on yours?

DOREEN: RB/57/212/X.

DORIS: (*Reading out another document*) RB/57/212/X.

DOREEN: (*Reading out another document*) RB/57/212/X.

DORIS: (*Reading out another document*) RB/57/212/X.

DOREEN: Doris.

DORIS: Doreen?

DOREEN: They're all from the same person. (*Pause*) Don't you feel chilly?

DORIS: (*Slowly*) Somebody's going mad.

(*Someone comes along the corridor talking and the door opens with difficulty. This is because the door-handle is broken. It is also because* LOMAX, *the office messenger, has only one arm. Another messenger,* BOSWELL, *who is silent and black, remains propped in the doorway while* LOMAX *unloads the incoming files from the trolley. It is to* BOSWELL *all* LOMAX'S *conversation is addressed.* DORIS *and* DOREEN *are ignored and they endeavour to ignore him too.*)

LOMAX: I said 'ASTMS?' He said 'Yes.' I said 'I've always assumed I was Transport and General Workers.' 'A common mistake' he said. Nice looking feller. Bit of a beard. Only young. I said 'ASTMS? That's Scientific, Technical and Managerial.' 'Mr Lomax,' he said (he knew my name), 'Full marks.' I said 'Well, for a kick-off I'm not Scientific. Furthermore I am not Technical, and in addition I am not Managerial.' He said 'Excuse me, friend, but haven't I seen you adjusting the thermostat for the central heating?' I said 'That is one of my functions.' 'Right' he said 'you're Scientific. Don't you on occasions man the lift?' 'Manually operated in cases of emergency, yes I do.' 'Right' he said 'you're Technical.' 'Do you have access to a telephone?' I said 'Yes.' 'Right' he said 'you're Managerial.' 'Frank,' he said (he knew my name), 'you shouldn't be in the TGWU, you. You, Frank, are hard-core ASTMS. You are what we call an ancillary worker.' I said 'Naturally, I shall want time to study

21

this one out. You're probably a political person. I vote, but that's about as far as it goes. Furthermore,' I said (I put my cards on the table), 'furthermore, I've frequently had occasion to vote Conservative.' 'Don't apologize, Frank' he said. 'It's a free country.' 'Whereas you,' I said, 'I don't know, but I imagine, just looking at you (and I don't mean the earring; my eldest lad wears one, married with a nice little milk-round in Doncaster) you are ... probably a militant.' 'Up to a point, Frank' he said. 'Yes.' So I said, 'Well let's get it quite straight at the outset, I have no sympathy for that at all. I fought in the Western Desert and I have no sympathy for that at all.' He went very quiet. He said, 'Frank. Let me ask you one question. Pay and Conditions. Satisfied or not satisfied?' 'Not satisfied.' I said. 'Nor are we.' he said! '*Nor are we*'. 'Can I ask you another question? Are you index linked?' 'Alas,' I said, 'No.' 'Top of the agenda, Frank' he said. 'Our No. 1 priority.' So I said, 'What about comparable facilities? TGWU has a very nice holiday home at Cleveleys.' He said, 'Have you ever been to Mablethorpe?' No. 'Frank,' he said, 'you've got a treat in store.'
(DORIS *and* DOREEN *have been steadfastly ignoring this conversation while attending to every word.* LOMAX *has been bringing in more and more work from the trolley. There is only one item on the Out tray, the green form.*)
Is this all there is to go? A green form. Staff and Appointments. Misrouted. Right hive of bloody industry this is. (*They ignore him.*) 'Anyway,' he said, 'I don't want to twist your arm, but there's a difficult time coming. There are storm clouds ahead, Frank. Big, black storm clouds. Putting it in simple economic terms, it's going to rain, Frank. It's not merely going to rain. It's going to piss it down. And some people, some people, are going to get wet.
(DOREEN *is plainly agitated by this conversation to which she is steadfastly not listening.*)
They are going to get so wet that they are going to be washed clean away. Washed down the drain. So if it's raining, Frank, what's the first thing you do? You get yourself an umbrella. And the ASTMS is that umbrella, the umbrella tailored to your needs. (LOMAX *is going.*) I see you have only one arm, Frank,' he said. 'One of the less publicized aspects of ASTMS activity is the provision of more facilities for the disabled. We've been pulling a lot of strings on that. What happened to your arm?' he said. 'Rommel,' I said. 'Who?' he said. 'Before your time,' I said. 'Tobruk. You probably saw the film.' 'Sorry, Frank,' he said, 'the film was before my

time too ... '

(LOMAX *goes out followed by* BOSWELL. *The door closes. Opens again.* DOREEN *gets up and closes it.*)

DOREEN: You'd think having one arm would make somebody nicer.
(DORIS *is consulting various manuals, looking for the reference number.*)
Blind people are nice. Nine times out of ten. And look at Mr Goldthorpe with the funny foot, he's lovely. But I wouldn't thank you for a union. Me and Cliff that's the only union I'm interested in.

DORIS: RB/57/212/X. RB is what? East Anglia?

DOREEN: (*Looking through the newly arrived post etc.*) Thames Valley.
Postcard here from Pauline Lucas.

DORIS: Thames Valley.

DOREEN: 'Dear Girls, Journey to Luton uneventful but a nice crowd on the plane. We are staying at this big new hotel on an unspoiled part of the Spanish coast. We have palled on with a couple from Birmingham.' (Or is it Billingham?) 'He is a comptometer operator and she is in fabrics. Tell Mr Cunliffe I miss him, I don't think. Vince sends his love but only a bit because in my present mood' (underlined) 'there isn't much to spare.' Exclamation mark. 'P.S. I think it's the garlic.' (*She pins it up.*) Good old Pauline. Always has a nice time.

DORIS: 57 is year of entry. Joined Thames Valley in 1957.

DOREEN: You don't think it's just somebody trying it on?

DORIS: Trying what on?

DOREEN: Well once upon a time when we were still in the old annexe I had ten 476s in the same day. I nearly went mad. Then I thought it might be somebody in Records, flirting.

DORIS: Funny way of flirting. 476s. 203s you could understand it.

DOREEN: You never know with Records, forms are all the same to them. They don't have the sweat of filling them out.

DORIS: And was it?

DOREEN: Was it what?

DORIS: Somebody flirting.

DOREEN: No. A bottleneck at Cardiff.

DORIS: It's somebody who was taken on in 1957 at Thames Valley. Now what's 212.

DOREEN: Doris.

DORIS: What?

DOREEN: There is an easier way. If that's her Personnel number, why not ring Personnel?
(*Pause*)

DORIS: Pick up the phone. Pick it up, Doreen. Ring. 'Hello, Personnel. Precepts and Invoices. Doreen Bidmead speaking. I wanted you to be the first to know: I have just plunged a knife into Doris Rutter's heart.' How can we ring Personnel? You may, Doreen, but I couldn't. It would stick in my throat.

DOREEN: What?

DORIS: The washbasin plug. They stole it, remember?

DOREEN: I was only thinking aloud.

(*Awkward pause.* DORIS *is all this time going through documents trying to decipher the Personnel number.*)

I still wonder about Mrs Henstridge. Didn't she have a daughter that was in an accident? I've a feeling the hat came round.

DORIS: They wouldn't send the hat round for her daughter. Her daughter never worked here.

DOREEN: They send the hat round for the famine victims. They don't work here.

DORIS: They send the hat round for all sorts these days. I hope they send the hat round for me when my turn comes. If it's not a wedding it's a famine. Earthquakes practically twice a week nowadays. Never stops. Ethiopia. What have we got to do with Ethiopia?

DOREEN: I just have this feeling I chipped in for a spray.

DORIS: Here we are. (*She finds the reference.*)

DOREEN: It's not called Ethiopia now is it. It's something else. All the names have changed. Africa. Ceylon. You don't know where you are. Why can't everything stay exactly the same all the time, that's my philosophy?

DORIS: Diana Bunce. Angela Barltrop. Deirdre Barnes. Dorcas Burns. Betty Brookes. (*Pause*) Dorothy Binns. Dorothy Binns.

DOREEN: Dorothy Binns.

DORIS: Dorothy Binns. RB/57/212/X is Dorothy Binns.

DOREEN: Do you know, I'm going to have to put my cardigan on.

(*The lights fade slowly down to indicate a brief passage of time. Up again.*)

DORIS: Dorothy Binns. (*Pause*) Dorothy Binns. (*Pause*) Dorothy Binns.

DOREEN: I wish you wouldn't keep saying 'Dorothy Binns'. Saying 'Dorothy Binns' isn't going to get us any further.

(*Pause*)

DORIS: Dorothy Binns. I've seen her name somewhere. I've seen it today. Dorothy Binns.

DOREEN: Can't we try and get some more gen instead of just sitting there saying her name? Saying her name. It gets on my nerves. Dorothy Binns.

(DORIS *looks through the forms.*)

DORIS: RB/57/212/X. Dorothy Binns.

DOREEN: Oh shut up about her. What's it matter anyway? I'm not going to just sit here all day saying Dorothy Binns. I'm getting on with some work.

(*Pause, while* DOREEN *starts to go through some of the papers* LOMAX *has delivered.*)

Doris.

DORIS: What?

DOREEN: I hardly like to say this.

DORIS: What?

DOREEN: I seem to have got some 104s too.

DORIS: How many?

DOREEN: Three.

DORIS: That makes six. I'm going mad. What's the Personnel number?

DOREEN: Same. The mystery woman.

DORIS: Dorothy Binns. Who is she?

(*Pause*)

DOREEN: Doris.

DORIS: What?

DOREEN: Why do we want to know all about her? (*Pause*) We could just fill in the forms and have done with it. It won't take all that long.

(*Pause*)

DORIS: You used to be such a bright girl. When I pulled you out of the typing pool. So *bright*. Only then you were just plain Doreen Allnatt. It's the Bidmead that's done it. You and Clifford stuck there all night. Nothing to talk about except forced rhubarb. Since when did that hone the mind? Winter sprouting broccoli. Course we want to know who it is, you silly article. This Miss Binns has suddenly landed us with a fistful of 104s. Who is she? Why's she doing it? Nobody bothers with 104s these days unless they're going by the book. If everybody started going by the book we'd be swamped. It's a change in work patterns, an increase in work load. I'm not having it. If you can't understand that, Mrs Bidmead, then you'd better stick to rhubarb.

(*Pause*)

DOREEN: Doris.

DORIS: What?

DOREEN: I know.

25

DORIS: Know what?

DOREEN: How we can find out about Dorothy Binns.

DORIS: How? And if you say try Personnel I'll staple your tits together.

DOREEN: (*Shocked*) Doris.

DORIS: I don't care. There's something happening here and I want to know what it is.

DOREEN: You might at least say Pardon my French.

DORIS: When?

DOREEN: If you say anything like that. Pardon my French.

DORIS: It isn't French.

DOREEN: Clifford says Pardon my French if he even says Bloody. (Pardon my French.)

DORIS: Good for Clifford. Well? You said you knew? How? How do we get the magic information? (*Pause*) All right. Pardon my French. (*Pause*)

DOREEN: It's a bit late now. (*Pause*) Try Tanya.

DORIS: Tanya who?

DOREEN: You never know anybody, do you? It's the sixth floor. 'Work has a human face.' Tanya Lockwood. At Garstang. The computer centre. Tall willowy girl. Them big glasses. Won a candlelit dinner for two in the productivity bonus scheme. (*She is telephoning.*) Hello, Garstang? Harrogate speaking. Precepts and Invoices. Mrs Bidmead. Tanya Lockwood please. Computer Centre. Oh? (She's been transferred.) To whom am I speaking? I don't believe it. I do not believe it. Is it really? Well isn't that *funny*. And then they say there isn't a God! (It's Mrs Henstridge.) How are you? We were just wondering where you'd got to. We're champion, you know, trundling along. Things don't change, do they? Tobago! Goodness. That's a far cry. (Her daughter's gone to the Solomon Islands.) And do you like it there? No, not the Solomon Islands, Garstang. (She loves it.) I imagine it is clean, yes, but I think I'd miss people, you know. People. *People*. (She says she knits a lot.) We were only saying this morning how you used to have sole responsibility for green forms. Do you remember when green forms went through you? They did go through you, didn't they? Oh, Newcastle. Not you. Oh well. Something went through you, because I remember. I was thinking it was going to be Tanya Lockwood. Tanya Lockwood. Thin girl. Big glasses. I wonder where she's gone. Listen I'll tell you why I'm ringing. We've got a little problem-ette here. Doris is saying to give you her love. (DORIS *isn't at all.*) Doris. Doris Rutter. Her mother had that bad hip. Lives at Meanwood.

26

She has a little Jack Russell, you remember. She sends her love.
(She sends it back.) We've got a little problem-ette here *vis à vis*
some PS104s. You can well laugh. We're not laughing I can tell you.
(*She is in fact.*) They all seem to emanate from someone by the name
of Dorothy Binns. We're trying to get some gen on her. Dorothy
Binns. We've got her Personnel Registration Number. We thought
of asking Mr Cunliffe in Personnel—yes, he can be charming when
it suits him but we have a little demarcation dispute with Personnel
at the moment to do with toilet requisites. What we wondered was if
you could just slip the name of this Miss Binns . . . well I'm saying
Miss she might be Mrs . . . into the computer and see what it comes
up with . . . in the way of her history with the group, present-day
location, and so on. Yes. (*Long pause.*) Yes. Yes. I do see that, yes.
(It's fully programmed for the next fortnight.) Yes. Yes. Couldn't
you perhaps slip it in during the lunch hour? No. I know it doesn't
have a lunch hour, but you do presumably. Unless Garstang's a very
different place from Harrogate. Ha Ha. No. (*Long pause.*) No. No.
Well never mind. We'll explore other avenues. Nice to have come
across you again. No. Don't work too hard. (*End of phone call. Long
silence.*) I can't believe it's the same woman. As soon as I mentioned
the computer she went right hard. Machines change people, I think.
Thin-faced woman. Blonde-ish. Had one of these poncho affairs.

DORIS: She reckoned to be your friend.

DOREEN: Oh no. I saw her in the lift once or twice, that's all. Sharpish
face. Now I think of it, her hair was probably dyed. Never mind.
(*Pause*)

DORIS: Dorothy Binns. (*Pause*) Dorothy Binns. (*Pause*) Dorothy Binns.

DOREEN: I think I'll just pay a visit.

DORIS: I've seen it somewhere today, I know.

DOREEN: (*Off*) What's that?

DORIS: I said I've seen it somewhere.

DOREEN: (*Off*) What?

DORIS: Dorothy *Binns*. (*She gets all the PS104s together.*) What did I do
this morning? (*Shouting to* DOREEN.) What did I do this morning? I
came in. I had some coffee.

DOREEN: (*Off*) You had some coffee.

DORIS: I looked through the post.

DOREEN: (*Off*) Telephoned Hazel about badminton.

DORIS: Telephoned Hazel about badminton. Cleared my In tray.

DOREEN: (*Off*) Read the paper.

DORIS: (*Slightly irritated that of all the things* DOREEN *remembers none are*

27

work) Read the paper. Stopped you sending that green Personnel form to Newcastle.

DOREEN: (*Off*) What?

DORIS: Was that it? The green Personnel form? No. Can't have been. I never even looked at it. I don't know. (*She starts going through the list of PS104s.*) One lampshade. One light bulb. One carpet runner. One waste-paper basket. One washbasin plug. One soap dispenser. One towel rail.

(DOREEN *appears at the door drying her hands.*)

DOREEN: What were those last ones again?

DORIS: One towel rail. One soap dispenser. One washbasin plug.

(DOREEN *looks back down the corridor to the toilet.*)

DOREEN: Go on with the list.

DORIS: One lampshade. One light bulb. One carpet runner.

(DOREEN *wanders about the office, locating each item as* DORIS *mentions it.*)

DOREEN: Doris. (DORIS *says nothing.*) Doris.

DORIS: What?

DOREEN: There's something funny about those 104s.

DORIS: We know that, closet. Otherwise why would I be sitting here, racking my brains? They all emanate from the same person. Dorothy Bloody Pardon my French Binns.

DOREEN: No. Besides that. Listen. One washbasin plug. One carpet runner. One waste-paper basket.

DORIS: Well.

DOREEN: Don't you see. One lampshade. One carpet runner. One light bulb. They're all items *we're* short of.

DORIS: They're all items any office in the North Western Area is short of.

(DOREEN *takes* DORIS *by the hand. Conducts her round the office pointing out the deficiencies.*)

DOREEN: One lampshade.

DORIS: One lampshade. (*Scornfully*)

DOREEN: One light bulb.

DORIS: One light bulb. (*Scornfully*)

DOREEN: One door-handle.

The door opens of its own accord and DORIS *absent-mindedly closes it.*)
One rubber plant. One carpet runner.

DORIS: One rubber plant. One carpet runner. No, no. Offices they're all the same.

DOREEN: One pane of glass.

DORIS: Well, one pane of glass ... (*One pane of glass is missing.*)

DOREEN: Three Venetian-blind slats.

DORIS: And three Venetian bl ... Let me look at those. No. (*Three Venetian-blind slats are missing from the blind.*) No.

DOREEN: It is, it is. Somebody's wanting to do up our office. Our office. Somebody else.

DORIS: No. I don't believe it.

DOREEN: It is.

DORIS: Why would anybody want to do that?

DOREEN: It's not anybody is it. It's the mystery woman. Dorothy Binns. Has it gone hot in here? I'm boiling. Where did you see the name, Doris? Think, Doris, think. (*She flings off her cardigan.*)

DORIS: I am thinking.

DOREEN: Nobody's ever been interested in us before have they? The annual inspection, that's all. Otherwise you'd hardly know we were here.

DORIS: She knows we're here.

DOREEN: Why? Why?

DORIS: Doreen. Doreen.

DOREEN: I know why. I know. It's redundancy, Doris. It's the cutbacks. Like in the *Bulletin*. Goodbye to Leeds Cardigan Road. Smiles and sadness at simple ceremony.

DORIS: That's it, the *Bulletin*. That's where I saw her name. I saw her name in the *Bulletin*. Dorothy Binns. Where is the bloody *Bulletin*?

DOREEN: Oh yes, yes. It doesn't matter about Pardon my French. Where is it?

(*They search frantically all over the office, scattering files on the floor, until eventually* DOREEN, *with a cry of discovery, runs the* Bulletin *to earth in the waste-paper basket.*)

DORIS: 'Newport Pagnell comes of age. Smiling graduates of the twenty-first computer course at Roker Park. Left to right. Gillian Smallbone (Portsmouth). Brian Priestly (Croydon, London Rd). Betty Butterfield (Stoke). R. Jack Fieldhouse (Sheffield). Dorothy Binns (Southport).'

DOREEN: And it says smiling. If that's her smiling what's the other like?

DORIS: Southport. Southport.

DOREEN: Southport's being wound down.

DORIS: Up. We still have those pink Personnel forms. Southport'll be in among them somewhere.

DOREEN: She has that hair I don't like either. I've never liked that sort of hair.

DORIS: Stockport, Stalybridge, Southampton. (*Working through the pink forms.*) Wolverhampton. What's Wolverhampton doing here?

DOREEN: It's because of Solihull.

DORIS: Stanmore, Southsea, Southport. Southport. (*She opens the folder.*) Bast, Barker, Barnett, Banerjee, Binns. Binns! I can't see. We need another light in this room.

(DOREEN *moans.*)

DOREEN: I know. And a carpet and a plant, and a washbasin plug and ...

DORIS: Doreen. Get a grip. Look. Look at her credits. She's been all over. Sheffield. Huddersfield. Norwich, Crewe.

DOREEN: All those have been wound up.

DORIS: Down.

DOREEN: Everywhere she's been, Doris, a trail of redundancy.

DORIS: Look at the courses. Manpower Services Course, Tewkesbury. Personnel Selection Course, Basingstoke. Time and Motion Study Course, Winchester ... Manpower Services Computerization Course, Andover. Time and Motion, Computerization, they're all different ways of spelling the same word. Redundancy.

DOREEN: Doris!

DORIS: Doreen!

DOREEN: And she's coming here. Here. And not only here. *Here*. *There*. (*The empty desk.*)

DORIS: We don't know for certain.

DOREEN: Those three Venetian-blind slats tell a different story.

DORIS: Why here? This is a highly qualified, go-ahead, ambitious woman.

DOREEN: I know, I know. I'm sweltering! (*She takes off her scarf.*)

DORIS: A woman with a long string of qualifications. Middle-management material. Sights set on higher echelons. Fifth-floor fodder. No. Not here. Except ...

DOREEN: Except what?

DORIS: Maybe that's how she likes to work. Under cover. Sussing the place out. Worming herself in ... then suddenly, ruthlessly ... the *knife*.

(DOREEN *shrieks and rushes into the lavatory.*)

I don't know why you're crying, you wet lettuce. You're married. You've got Clifford. I've only got Mother. She doesn't bring much in.

DOREEN: (*From the loo*) They must redeploy us. They redeployed people at Southport.

DORIS: Did they hell! Where do they redeploy people at Southport?

30

What do they redeploy them as? Deck-chair attendants? Donkey men? Rubbish.

DOREEN: What?

DORIS: Rubbish. It's the SACK. Henceforth we'll just have to plan on redeploying ourselves down to the Labour Exchange.

(DOREEN *emerges. To find* DORIS *has calmed down and is preparing to start work.*)

DOREEN: Oh, Doris, Thank God for Clifford's smallholding.

DORIS: Just what I was thinking.

DOREEN: Why?

DORIS: Well I imagine the lay-offs will be selective.

DOREEN: Selective?

DORIS: The usual principle. Last in, first out. Done by grades.

DOREEN: Grades. Me?

(*Pause*)

DORIS: Yes.

DOREEN: You?

DORIS: No.

(DORIS *begins to work at her desk. Pause.*)

DOREEN: What are you doing, Doris?

DORIS: Oh, I just thought I'd get on with these pink forms for Mr Cunliffe. I don't seem to have made much progress with them somehow today.

DOREEN: *Quelle bonne idée.* Bung me a few over. I'll do one or two. Many hands!

DORIS: No trouble honestly. Old Doris can manage. Eazy peazy. I hope the day hasn't dawned when Doris Rutter can't cope with a few measly old Personnel forms.

DOREEN: Don't think little Doreen's casting any nasturtiums, but as the proverb has it, every little helps. I can do pink forms with the old eyes closed.

DORIS: I know that. Who can't?

DOREEN: The sooner we're finished, the sooner we're done.

DORIS: You could straighten up.

DOREEN: Doreen? Straighten up? I don't think it was Doreen made the mess, was it? (*She addresses the chaos.*) Was it, papers? Was it Doreen pulled you all out and threw you on the floor? No, it wasn't, was it? Who was it, then? Who was it made such a mess? Was it her? Yes.

DORIS: Better not let the sixth floor hear you talking like that or you'll end up like Miss Batty. Looking after your brother in Rhyl.

DOREEN: I don't have a brother in Rhyl. I don't have a brother. You
won't let me do pink forms. I've got to do something.

DORIS: Tidy up. Ready for Miss Binns.

DOREEN: Yes. That would suit you, wouldn't it. My tidying up, you
typing. I'm not one of these ancillary workers. I'm skilled.

DORIS: Semi-skilled.

DOREEN: Skilled.

DORIS: Grade 4.

DOREEN: Grade 3.

DORIS: Only substantively.

DOREEN: Gradings can alter.

DORIS: Not when they're frozen. You are Grade 4 semi-skilled, ancillary,
so clear up that mess, Mrs Bidmead, before Miss Binns comes and
finds the place a pigsty.

(DOREEN *starts tidying up.*)

DOREEN: Don't Mrs Bidmead me. I don't wonder you've never got
married. Domineering. You'd domineer Goering, you would.
Mother! Mother! Mother's just an excuse. Somebody look twice at
you, you'd soon cart her off to the gerry ward.

DORIS: And she knitted you those dishcloths!

DOREEN: It's you I'm talking about, not her.

DORIS: I got you on to her list. She's got several people waiting for them.
You got preferential treatment. Does that sound like Goering?

DOREEN: I've nothing against your Mother.

DORIS: I should think not. You've never met her.

DOREEN: I feel as if I had. I never hear about anybody else.

DORIS: I don't talk about Mother.

DOREEN: You do.

DORIS: I don't.

DOREEN: Listen. She spent half the night on the commode. How do I
know that? It wasn't in the *Yorkshire Post*. You think you've got a
mother monopoly, you. Other people have mothers. Clifford has a
mother.

DORIS: Clifford's mother hasn't got a plastic hip.

DOREEN: He wouldn't broadcast it if she had. Anyway, what are plastic
hips these day? There's all sorts with plastic hips. Cabinet ministers.
Disc jockeys. Even proper jockeys. It's not a handicap any more.
People who've had experience of them prefer them to real ones. And
what about me? I'm not strong. But of course we never talk about
that. Because I'm a Grade 4, semi-skilled ancillary worker. Semi-
skilfully clearing up all this skilful Grade 3 mess. You've done it on

32

me, Doris.

DORIS: I haven't done it on you, Doreen. It's Personnel. They've done it on both of us. It's Mr Cunliffe that's done it on us. The nasty little tripehound. Dorothy Binns!

DOREEN: I shall be redundant. Surplus to requirements. Little Doreen Allnatt. All those years ago. Pulled out of the typing pool. For what? Redeployment. Redundancy. The scrap heap.

DORIS: Oh, Doreen, I'm sorry.

DOREEN: Don't touch me. Don't even speak to me. (*She weeps.*)

DORIS: Oh, Doreen. Doreen.

(*Enter* LOMAX.

DORIS's *manner instantly changes, whereas* DOREEN *remains the same, still tidying up, crying as she does it.*)

LOMAX: What's up with her? What's the matter, love?

DORIS: It's nothing. Her mother-in-law's poorly.

DOREEN: (*Stops instantly*) She never is.

LOMAX: Boadicea been giving you the treatment?

DORREN: No. I'm upset.

LOMAX: What about?

DORIS: Don't expose yourself, Doreen. That will be all.

LOMAX: Personnel want those pink forms.

DORIS: Give Mr Cunliffe my compliments and tell him Miss Rutter will let him have the forms by four o'clock at the latest.

DOREEN: And Mrs Bidmead.

DORIS: Just say Miss Rutter is completing them now.

DOREEN: And Mrs Bidmead. Say Mrs Bidmead. Else this new Miss Binns will think I'm just another ancillary worker. She won't let me near a typewriter even.

LOMAX: Nothing wrong with being an ancillary worker. I'm an ancillary worker. I'm laughing.

DOREEN: Why?

LOMAX: I've just got under the umbrella. The ASTMS.

DOREEN: I'm not in the union at all.

LOMAX: Then come on under quick.

DORIS: Doreen.

DOREEN: Why not?

DORIS: We've always been opposed to unionization.

DOREEN: We! We. I'm an ancillary worker. I'm Grade 4 .You're Grade 3.

DORIS: Remember the Tolpuddle Martyrs.

LOMAX: What grade were they?

DOREEN: My grading's frozen.

LOMAX: No problem. Object No. 1 of the ASTMS, index linking. Objective No. 2, thawing gradings. I'll give my friend a tinkle. He'll be round like a shot. You'll like him. Very gentle. Soft spoken. Little beard.

DORIS: Little beard!

LOMAX: Shall I?

DOREEN: Yes. Yes, ring him. Tell him I'm interested.

DORIS: Doreen. Don't lower yourself.

DOREEN: Damn you, Doris.

(LOMAX *is going*.)

LOMAX: Girls, girls, girls. Who is it's supposed to be coming? Miss who?

DOREEN: Binns. Dorothy Binns.

LOMAX: Never heard of her. No Miss Binns here.

(*He looks at his clipboard*.)

DOREEN: She's in the offing.

LOMAX: No.

DOREEN: She is.

DORIS: Doreen.

LOMAX: Listen. We've got a Miss Bird coming into Costing and Estimates. Mr Bottomley into Accounts and Mr Sharples into Maintenance but no Miss Binns.

DOREEN: Are you sure?

LOMAX: Do I know everything that goes on in this group or don't I? There is no Miss Binns. Anyway, I'll telephone my friend.

DOREEN: (*Uncertainly*) Well, perhaps—

LOMAX: You want to get in, girl. Get in while there's still room under the umbrella.

(LOMAX *goes*. *Silence*.)

DORIS: I think you'll live to regret that, Doreen.

DOREEN: You forced me into it. Ancillary worker. I'm not an ancillary worker. Only technically anyway. (*Pause*) He'd never heard of Miss Binns had he?

DORIS: No.

DOREEN: Doris. Are there some of those 5D forms left?

DORIS: One or two.

DOREEN: Could I do them?

DORIS: If you like.

DOREEN: Oh, Doris. (*Pause*) I'm sorry I said that about Mother.

DORIS: What?

DOREEN: About Goering and the dishcloths.

34

DORIS: It was nothing. Doreen.

DOREEN: Doris.

DORIS: You won't be seeing this union person?

DOREEN: Nothing to see him about really, is there, Doris? If this Binns woman's not coming.

DORIS: Oh she's not coming. I know that for certain. It came to me when our friend was here. Of course he hasn't heard of her. If this Dorothy Binns was coming here, to our little office, what would be the first thing we would get?

(DORIS *picks up the manual as* DOREEN *shakes her head.*)

Look at the procedure. Selection and Appointments, North Western Area. Newcastle, Triad House. All communication on a district level to be routed through Area Staff and Selection with contingency copies to records and *relevant departments concerned*, i.e. us. If this lady were headed in our direction we would have been notified of the fact by a green form. We haven't had a green form. Therefore she is not coming. Procedure, you see, Doreen, it can be a tyrant. It can set you free. So *relaxez vous*, Doreen. Let it all hang out. We haven't had a green Personnel form. She is not coming. So much for Miss Dorothy Binns!

(*Pause. Then* DOREEN *slowly puts her cardigan on.*)

DOREEN: Doris.

DORIS: What?

DOREEN: We have.

DORIS: Have what?

DOREEN: Had a green form. We had one first thing. The one I thought went through Mrs Henstridge. Only you said it had nothing to do with us because we weren't a relevant department concerned. You sent it down to Staff and Appointments, Mr Titmuss.

DORIS: Doreen. If we were the relevant department concerned, Mr Titmuss would have sent it straight back. He hasn't, has he?

DOREEN: No. Sorry, Doris.

(*At this point the door opens,* LOMAX *pops his head round and puts a form in the correspondence tray.*)

LOMAX: ASTMS. Doesn't stop you being a bloody yo-yo.

(*He goes. Silence.*)

DORIS: Doreen.

DOREEN: Yes, Doris.

DORIS: Is that from Staff and Appointments?

DOREEN: Yes, Doris.

DORIS: Is it a green form?

DOREEN: Yes, Doris.

DORIS: Is there a note from Mr Titmuss?

DOREEN: Yes, Doris.

DORIS: Read it, Doreen.

DOREEN: 'Doris, pet. Somebody up there in Precepts and Invoices wants their bottom smacking. This isn't our baby at all. Phew, exclamation mark! You gave us quite a turn. Don't *do* that sort of thing. We like to sleep in the mornings. Stan.'

DORIS: Open it. What's the Personnel number?

DOREEN: RB/57.

DORIS: (*Joins in*) /212/X.

DORIS: Dorothy Binns.

DOREEN: Ms Dorothy Binns. Ms. She's one of them, too. Still, she may not stay long.

DORIS: She didn't stay anywhere long. Crewe, Chesterfield, Lytham, Southport. All wound up.

DOREEN: Down.

DORIS: Out. Personnel. They're the ones. They've done it on us, Doreen.

DOREEN: This will be her desk.

DORIS: She probably sat at it this morning. Before we came in. What time did we come in?

DOREEN: Half-past nine-ish.

DORIS: That'll stop.

DOREEN: I'm so cold.

DORIS: It's locked. That means she's brought her stuff already. The nerve. Locking her desk. The cheeky cow. She's never even met us and already she doesn't trust us. I don't lock my desk.

DOREEN: I don't lock mine.

DORIS: We've got nothing to hide.

DOREEN: We trust each other.

DORIS: She doesn't.

DOREEN: What has she got to hide?

DORIS: We'll soon find out. I'm having this open.

DOREEN: How?

DORIS: The usual way. (*She cuts a slat from the already depleted Venetian blind and uses it to insert in the crack in the desk drawer and picks the lock.*) It's all very neat.

DOREEN: An apple.

DORIS: That means she doesn't have lunch.

DOREEN: Oh, Doris, I'm frightened. Look at the point on those pencils!

DORIS: A name plate. Yes. Dorothy Binns.

(DOREEN *has picked out a framed document, which she reads.*)

DOREEN: Listen to this:

'I am the foundation of all business.
I am the source of all prosperity.
I am the parent of genius.
I am the salt that gives life its savour.
I am the foundation of every fortune.
I do more to advance youth than parents, be they never so wealthy.
I must be loved before I can bestow my greatest blessings, and
achieve my greatest ends.
Loved I can make life sweet, purposeful and fruitful.
I am represented in the most limited savings, the largest body of
investments.
All progress springs from me.
What am I?'

(*An ominous figure stands in the doorway casting a black shadow across
the stage.*)

MS BINNS: I am Work. I am Work.

A Visit from Miss Prothero

ARTHUR DODSWORTH
MISS PROTHERO

The living-room of a semi-detached house. A worn, comfortable, cosy place.
Dozing in an armchair and similarly worn, cosy and comfortable is MR
DODSWORTH, *a man in his sixties. In a cardigan and carpet slippers with the top*
button of his trousers undone MR DODSWORTH *is retired. He is just having five*
minutes and, unless one counts the budgie, he is alone.
A few moments pass, sufficient for the tranquillity of the household to be
established, then the door-chimes go.
MR DODSWORTH *does not respond.*
The chimes go again.
MR DODSWORTH *stirs and fastening the top button of his trousers gets up and*
addresses the budgie.

MR DODSWORTH: Who's this then, Millie? Who's this?
    (*He goes out, leaving the living-room door open. The front door opens.*)
    (*Off*) Is it you, Miss Prothero?
MISS PROTHERO: (*Off*) It is.
MR DODSWORTH: (*Off*) I didn't expect to see you.
    (*While* DODSWORTH *hovers in the living-room doorway the visitor comes*
    in boldly. It is a middle-aged woman, who runs a critical eye over the
    warm, comfortable, cosy room. She is none of these things.)
MISS PROTHERO: I was beginning to think I'd got the wrong house.
MR DODSWORTH: Why? Had you been stood there long?
MISS PROTHERO: A minute or two.
MR DODSWORTH: No, it's the right house. Number 59. The Dodsworth
    residence.
MISS PROTHERO: I rang twice.
MR DODSWORTH: To tell you the truth I was just having five minutes.
MISS PROTHERO: I'm surprised. You were the one who couldn't abide a
    nap.
MR DODSWORTH: Was I? You'll take your coat off?
MISS PROTHERO: I was waiting to be asked.
    (*He starts to help her off with her coat.*)
    I shan't stop.
MR DODSWORTH: No, but ...

MISS PROTHERO: I still have my back, so I'll keep my undercoat on.
(MR DODSWORTH *is tugging at her cardigan sleeve, trying to take it off.*)
That's my undercoat.
MR DODSWORTH: Sorry. Sorry.
MISS PROTHERO: This time of year can be very treacherous.
(*Spring, summer, autumn, winter . . . to* MISS PROTHERO *the seasons were all potential assassins.*)
And I'd best keep my hat on as well. I don't want another sinus do.
(MR DODSWORTH *is about to bear away the fainted form of* MISS PROTHERO's *swagger coat when she stops him.*)
I'm forgetting my hanky.
(*She takes it out of the pocket and blows her nose as* MR DODSWORTH *carries her coat out to the hallstand.*)
There's half a dozen people I ought to go see only I thought you might be feeling a bit out of it. I said to Doreen, 'I know Mr Dodsworth, he'll be wanting to be brought up to date.'
MR DODSWORTH: (*Off*) What on?
MISS PROTHERO: What on? Work! Warburtons!
MR DODSWORTH: (*Off*) Oh, *work*. No. No.
MISS PROTHERO: (*to herself*) I'm sorry I came then.
(*She remains standing in one spot, surveying the room as* DODSWORTH *bustles back.*)
MR DODSWORTH: What I mean, of course, is I do want to be brought up to date but to tell you the truth, Peggy, since I've left I've hardly had time to turn round. What with bowling on Tuesdays and my Rotary thing on Fridays and Gillian and the kiddies bobbing in every five minutes, I honestly haven't given work a thought. Which is amazing when you think I was there all those years. But you know what they say: retirement, it's a full-time job. Ha ha.
(MISS PROTHERO *doesn't laugh. She vaguely flinches.* MISS PROTHERO *is one of those people who only see jokes by appointment.*)
What about you? Have you taken the day off?
MISS PROTHERO: Mr Dodsworth, when did I take a day off? In all the years we worked together when did I ever take a day off? Even the day I buried Mother I came in in the afternoon to do the backlog. It shows you how out of touch you are. What day is it?
MR DODSWORTH: Thursday.
MISS PROTHERO: What week? Week 35. The Works Outing.
MR DODSWORTH: Are we into week 35? There you are. It just shows you how I've lost track. You've not gone then?
MISS PROTHERO: After last year? I haven't.

MR DODSWORTH: Is it Bridlington again?

MISS PROTHERO: Langdale Pikes.

MR DODSWORTH: A beauty spot! That's a departure. It's generally always Bridlington. Or thereabouts. Langdale Pikes. Quite scenic.

MISS PROTHERO: That's because Design put their spoke in. Costing and Estimates pulled a long face but it's only fair: it goes by departments. I dread to think where they'll choose next year.

MR DODSWORTH: Whose turn is it then?

MISS PROTHERO: (*Ominously*) Maintenance and Equipment. Mind you, as I said to Mr Butterfield in Projects, with a coachload of animals the venue is immaterial.

MR DODSWORTH: It's only once a year.

MISS PROTHERO: That coach, if it stopped once it stopped several times. Mr Teasdale's never looked me in the eye since. Wendy Walsh won't even speak to him.

MR DODSWORTH: I never thought he had it in him.

MISS PROTHERO: He was a wild beast. It's Mrs Teasdale I feel sorry for. Married to him. And she only has one kidney. Anyway Mr Skinner soon sized him up. He kept him filling out 5D forms the whole of the first week: that took the wind out of his sails. I thought 'Full marks to Mr Skinner.'

MR DODSWORTH: Oh yes, Skinner. How is Skinner?

MISS PROTHERO: Getting into his stride. I think he'll turn out to be a bit of a dynamo.

MR DODSWORTH: He seemed a nice fellow. Young, but nice. Aren't you going to sit down?

MISS PROTHERO: I was waiting to be asked.

(*She settles herself in a chair by the fire.*)

No. Don't you worry about Mr Skinner.

MR DODSWORTH: I wasn't.

MISS PROTHERO: He wouldn't thank you if you did. He goes his own way does Mr Skinner. Our new broom! All I wonder is how someone of his calibre bothers wasting his time at Warburtons. He could go anywhere, Mr Skinner. Brazil. New York. They'd snap him up.

(*On a table by where she is sitting is a wedding photograph.*)

Is that Mrs Dodsworth?

MR DODSWORTH: Which?

MISS PROTHERO: This woman with her arm through yours.

MR DODSWORTH: We'd just got married.

MISS PROTHERO: Oh. I suppose that's why she's smiling. Funny dress.

MR DODSWORTH: Is it? They're coming back now.

43

MISS PROTHERO: Like that? Are they? I haven't seen them. No, I was saying, it's not that I'm short of somewhere to go. I've got one or two people who're always begging me to pop in, one of them a retired chiropodist, but I knew you'd be wanting all the latest gen from Warburtons. I'd have come sooner but it's been a busy time, as you can imagine.

MR DODSWORTH: What with?

MISS PROTHERO: With the change-over. The new regime. I just bobbed on a bus. With the 23 going right up Gelderd Road it makes it very handy. You can tell; I was coming out of the house at twenty-five to and it's only ten past now.

MR DODSWORTH: You must have been lucky.

MISS PROTHERO: It's just a matter of pitching it right. Don't think I've ever had to wait for a bus, ever.

MR DODSWORTH: I've started pottery classes.

MISS PROTHERO: Whatever for?

MR DODSWORTH: I made this last week.

MISS PROTHERO: Oh. What is it?

MR DODSWORTH: It's an ash tray.

MISS PROTHERO: I didn't think you smoked. You wouldn't recognize the office now. There's all sorts been happening.

MR DODSWORTH: There has to me. I'm starting cooking classes.

MISS PROTHERO: Cookery? For men?

MR DODSWORTH: For anybody. There's several of us retired people, it's a right nice young lady does the teaching. It's Cordon Bleu.

MISS PROTHERO: Cordon Bleu!

MR DODSWORTH: I thought it was about time I branched out a bit.

MISS PROTHERO: I can see I've come to the wrong place. I thought you'd be busting for news of Warburtons and here you are all set up with pottery and cookery, out and about every night. We must seem very dull.

MR DODSWORTH: No, Peggy, you're wrong. You don't. But the way I look at it is this: I spent half my life at Warburtons and apart from Winnie it was my whole world. I've been retired four months and I'm beginning to see it's *not* the whole world, not by a long chalk. I was there thirty years, it's time I branched out.

MISS PROTHERO: Well, there you are, you say it's not the whole world: I got three letters last week from Japan, there was a firm enquiry from Zambia and Mr Skinner says once we get a foothold in these oil-producing countries, there's no reason why the whole of the Middle East shouldn't be banging on the door.

44

MR DODSWORTH: At Warburtons? Really?

MISS PROTHERO: We had a delegation round last week from Rumania.

MR DODSWORTH: They'd come a long way.

MISS PROTHERO: Mr Skinner introduced me. Considering they were from behind the Iron Curtain, I found them very charming.

MR DODSWORTH: What do they want coming round from Rumania?

MISS PROTHERO: We've got Mr Skinner to thank for that. He's a leading light in the Chamber of Trade. He says Warburtons is part of a much wider world picture. Export or die. And he runs that office with the smoothness of a well-oiled machine. Not that I'm saying you didn't.

MR DODSWORTH: Well, it was friendly.

MISS PROTHERO: Yes. He's put a stop to all that.

MR DODSWORTH: What?

MISS PROTHERO: All that going to the toilet. Mr Teasdale falling out for a smoke. Pauline Lucas coming down for half an hour at a stretch. He soon had her taped.

MR DODSWORTH: Is she still ginger?

MISS PROTHERO: Who?

MR DODSWORTH: Pauline. She was blonde. I thought ginger suited her better.

MISS PROTHERO: I thought it was a bit on the common side. And there's not so much of the Pauline nowadays either. People get called by their proper titles. It's Miss Prothero, Mrs Lucas. None of this Pauline and Peggying. Status. I like it.

(*Suddenly* MISS PROTHERO *lunges for the electric fire.*)

Could we have a bar off? Miss Cardwell's had her baby.

MR DODSWORTH: Who?

MISS PROTHERO: Miss Cardwell. In the typing pool.

MR DODSWORTH: Maureen? Had a baby? I thought she had rheumatic fever. In Nottingham.

MISS PROTHERO: Well if she did she got it knitting bootees.

MR DODSWORTH: Boy?

MISS PROTHERO: Girl. The image of him, so I'm told.

MR DODSWORTH: Who?

MISS PROTHERO: Mr Corkery.

MR DODSWORTH: In despatch?

MISS PROTHERO: Costing. He's been transferred.

MR DODSWORTH: Poor Maureen.

MISS PROTHERO: Poor nothing. She waltzed down with some snaps of it last week. I didn't know where to put myself.

45

MR DODSWORTH: Will she keep it?

MISS PROTHERO: She'll keep it all right. Same as Christine Thoseby kept hers. Park it in the day nursery all day and come in dressed up to the nines. Equal pay! They don't deserve it. I ran into her the other day, Christine. Yellow cashmere costume, high boots. That's the trouble these days: people don't know where to draw the line.

(*Pause*)

Food in the canteen doesn't get any better, mince three times last week. Somebody's making something on the side, meals that price. You never see that supervisor but what she's got a parcel. Wicked. If I were the fifth floor that's where I'd clamp down.

MR DODSWORTH: They always seem to have a smile, that's the main thing.

MISS PROTHERO: Of course they have a smile. Something to smile about, the money they make. That supervisor's just gone and got herself a little bungalow at Roundhay.

(MR DODSWORTH *doesn't want to know about the canteen, mince on the menu or the supervisor's bungalow at Roundhay. He doesn't want to know about Warburtons at all. There were worlds elsewhere. He goes over to the birdcage.*)

MR DODSWORTH: You haven't met Millie, have you? This is Miss Prothero. Say how do you do.

(*Millie doesn't oblige.*)

She's been a bit depressed today.

(*But* MISS PROTHERO *is not to be turned aside by the state of mind of an unknown budgie.*)

MISS PROTHERO: I wasn't aware they got depressed. What've they got to be depressed about? They don't have to work for a living.

(*Pause*)

I've changed my extension.

MR DODSWORTH: Oh yes?

MISS PROTHERO: You remember I used to be 216. Now I'm 314.

MR DODSWORTH: Going up in the world.

MISS PROTHERO: Doreen Glazier's 216 now. Big change for her. Preston and Fosters rang last week and didn't realize. I saw Mr Skinner smile. She's still got that nasty eczema.

MR DODSWORTH: Doreen? Poor girl.

MISS PROTHERO: The doctor thinks it's nerves. I think it's those tights. Man-made fibres don't do for everybody: I pay if I wear crimplene. But Doreen's never really been happy since her transfer. I ran into Miss Brunskill in the lift and she says when Doreen was in Credit and Settlement she was a different person. How old do you think she

46

is now?

MR DODSWORTH: Doreen?

MISS PROTHERO: Miss Brunskill.

MR DODSWORTH: Fifty?

MISS PROTHERO: Forty-eight, I was surprised. I saw it on her 253. I
thought she was nearer sixty. That's with being on the fifth floor. It
takes it out of you.

(MR DODSWORTH *is restive and bored.*)

MR DODSWORTH: Could you drink a cup of tea?

MISS PROTHERO: Tea? With my kidneys?

MR DODSWORTH: I forgot.

MISS PROTHERO: I wish I could forget. Tea—you might as well offer me
hydrocholoric acid.

MR DODSWORTH: Well, coffee?

MISS PROTHERO: Only if it's very weak.

(MR DODSWORTH *gets up and is on his way out.*)
How are your waterworks?

MR DODSWORTH: Sorry?

MISS PROTHERO: You were having a spot of trouble with your
waterworks, don't you remember?

MR DODSWORTH: They're champion now, thanks very much.

(MR DODSWORTH *thankfully leaves the room to put the kettle on.* MISS
PROTHERO *bides her time.*)

MISS PROTHERO: (*Calling*) And do you still have your appliance? (*There is
no answer.*) Is it still playing you up?

MR DODSWORTH: (*Off*) I never think about it now.

MISS PROTHERO: (*Still calling*) Typical of this country. Can't even make a
truss. (*She says the dreadful word with a kind of triumph.*)

MR DODSWORTH: (*Off*) Sugar?

MISS PROTHERO: If there is any.

(MR DODSWORTH *returns.*)

MR DODSWORTH: We're just waiting of the kettle.

MISS PROTHERO: In which case, if you don't mind, I think I'll pay a
call.

MR DODSWORTH: It's up on the landing. Facing you as you go up.

(*He listens as she goes upstairs, opens the door of the toilet and bolts it
after her.*)
Then get off home you bad, boring bitch.

(*He goes over to the birdcage.*)
What does she want to come on round here for in the first place?
We're quite happy, aren't we, Millie? Aren't we? We're quite

47

happy.

(*He gets out a little table and two plates as the toilet is flushed.* MISS PROTHERO *returns and* MR DODSWORTH *goes out as she comes in, saying cryptically . . .*)

Kettle.

(*While he makes coffee in the kitchen* MISS PROTHERO *looks critically at the mantelpiece.*)

MISS PROTHERO: Is this your clock?

MR DODSWORTH: (*Off*) Yes. It's a nice one, don't you think?

(MISS PROTHERO *shouts some of this to the kitchen. Other remarks she makes to herself.*)

MISS PROTHERO: Quite honestly I was against that. I spoke up when it was first mooted. Well I felt I had to. Time to give someone a clock is at the start of his career not the end. I said anyway. What do you want to know the time for, sat here? Time dribbling away and nothing to look forward to. Tick-tock tick-tock. It would get on my nerves.

MR DODSWORTH: (*Off*) It's not got a tick. It's electric.

MISS PROTHERO: You've still got the hands going round. It saves winding, I suppose.

(MR DODSWORTH *returns with a tray, two cups and some cake.*)

MR DODSWORTH: There's more to a clock than time. It's a memento. It makes me think back.

MISS PROTHERO: You were saying just now you didn't want to think back.

MR DODSWORTH: Well I do and I don't. You know how it is.

MISS PROTHERO: My proposal was something useful. An electric blanket.

MR DODSWORTH: Yes, only I like the inscription. You couldn't inscribe a blanket.

MISS PROTHERO: You were lucky it wasn't a rosebowl. Another useless article.

MR DODSWORTH: Cake? It's our Gillian's.

(*In* MISS PROTHERO'S *eyes this is no recommendation.*)

MISS PROTHERO: Just a small piece. No. Half that.

MR DODSWORTH: Winnie and I were given a canteen of cutlery when we were first married. It's stood us in good stead. See. Cake knives, everything. (*He displays the battery of cutlery and selects her a cake knife.*)

MISS PROTHERO: I can manage. They're only to wash up.

(MISS PROTHERO *drinks her coffee like medicine, every swallow loud, cavernous and unignorable.* MR DODSWORTH *flees to the sideboard, then to the birdcage.*)

What was Millie like?

48

MR DODSWORTH: Millie?

MISS PROTHERO: Millie. Mrs Dodsworth.

MR DODSWORTH: *Winnie*. Millie's the budgie.

MISS PROTHERO: I mean Winnie. (*Pause*) What was she like?

MR DODSWORTH: Well ... very nice. She was very nice. She was a saint. A real saint. (*Pause*) Pretty. When she was younger. Full of life. Not very practical.

MISS PROTHERO: Women aren't.

MR DODSWORTH: Though she rigged this place out. There was nothing here, nothing. She did all this herself, curtains and covers. She could make a place cosy could Winnie. She used to read a lot. Read all sorts. Naomi Jacob. Leo Walmsley. Phyllis Bentley. The Brontës. She'd read them all.

MISS PROTHERO: I suppose it's very nice if you've got the time. Me, I never open a book from one year's end to the next. Anyway, it's all escape.

MR DODSWORTH: I don't know it was with Win.

MISS PROTHERO: Oh yes, travel, romance. The mind's elsewhere. She'd be a bit lonely here all day, you at Warburtons. She never went out to work?

MR DODSWORTH: Well, she'd got our Gillian to look after. But she did all sorts. Rugs, crochet. These mats are hers. She never saw the clock. I'd have liked her to see the clock. What about your family?

MISS PROTHERO: My what?

MR DODSWORTH: Family.

MISS PROTHERO: Do you mean Father?

MR DODSWORTH: Oh yes. I'm sorry. Your mother died.

MISS PROTHERO: She didn't die. Father killed her.

MR DODSWORTH: Oh?

(*This is not the response* MISS PROTHERO *is after.*
Pause)

That's news to me.

MISS PROTHERO: Over forty-two years of marriage, slowly, day by day, inch by inch, smiling and smiling in the sight of the whole world, gently and politely with every appearance of kindness, he killed her. (*There is an endless pause.*)

MR DODSWORTH: What did he do for a living?

MISS PROTHERO: He was a gents' outfitter.

MR DODSWORTH: Really?

MISS PROTHERO: It was Other Women.

MR DODSWORTH: Oh ay.

MISS PROTHERO: In droves.

> (*What lives other people led. A gents' outfitter in Leeds with droves of Other Women. And he had hardly lived at all, thought* DODSWORTH.)

MR DODSWORTH: What was he like?

MISS PROTHERO: Tall. Little tash. A limp.

MR DODSWORTH: A limp?

MISS PROTHERO: Mother always said that helped. They felt safe.

> (*Women have always felt safe with me, thinks* MR DODSWORTH. *But then they were.* MISS PROTHERO *obviously feels quite safe. But then she is.*)

MR DODSWORTH: Is he still living?

MISS PROTHERO: Oh yes. He's had a stroke. He's in a home at Farnley. Paralysed all down one side. They have to do everything for him. Sits and sits and sits.

MR DODSWORTH: Still. He has his memories.

> (*Yes,* MISS PROTHERO *thinks, of Other Women.*)

MISS PROTHERO: Once he got taken for Ronald Colman.

MR DODSWORTH: Who?

MISS PROTHERO: Father.

MR DODSWORTH: Did Ronald Colman limp?

MISS PROTHERO: No, but he had a tash.

> (MR DODSWORTH *thinks of old Mr Prothero, paralysed all down one side up at Farnley, sat with his memories of droves of Other Women and once having been taken for Ronald Colman.*)

MR DODSWORTH: It doesn't paralyse the memory, then, a stroke?

MISS PROTHERO: Why?

MR DODSWORTH: It leaves you with half your movements. I wondered whether it left you with half your memories.

MISS PROTHERO: Well you wouldn't know, would you? If you can't remember it, how do you know you've forgotten it?

> (MR DODSWORTH *tries to bend his mind round this, fails and falls back on Art.*)

MR DODSWORTH: Do you fancy a bit of music?

MISS PROTHERO: I don't mind.

MR DODSWORTH: Do you not like music?

MISS PROTHERO: I don't mind. If it's played I listen to it.

MR DODSWORTH: That's something else I might take up. Musical appreciation. They have classes in that.

MISS PROTHERO: I don't care for the violin. Not on its own.

MR DODSWORTH: I think you'll like this. I do.

> (*He puts a cassette in the player. It is the theme from* Un Homme et Une Femme. *It goes on and on and on.* MISS PROTHERO *sits awkwardly*

50

waiting while MR DODSWORTH *listens appreciatively. She gives it a minute or two before deciding it's time to break the spell, which she does by suddenly getting to her feet.*)

MISS PROTHERO: They've introduced music in the lifts now. That was Mr Skinner's suggestion. It's industrial psychology. Is that clock fast?

MR DODSWORTH: No.

MISS PROTHERO: I was thinking of catching the twenty past.

MR DODSWORTH: Oh yes. (*He turns off the music.*)

MISS PROTHERO: But I've a bit yet.

(*She sits down again. Pause*)

I like to get back before dark. Two women attacked on the 73 last week. You'd never get me upstairs. It's just asking for it.

(*Pause*)

I don't seem to have told you much news. Mind you, if I told you everything that had been going on I don't suppose you'd thank me.

MR DODSWORTH: Well you have. You've brought me up to date on Maureen's baby. Doreen's skin trouble. It's just put me in the picture a bit. It's all I want.

MISS PROTHERO: That's only the half of it.

MR DODSWORTH: Perhaps, Peggy. But you see, it's this way. I was with Warburtons thirty years. Thirty years that saw big changes, some, I flatter myself, the work of yours truly. And doubtless the next thirty years will be the same. More changes. Except now it's somebody else's turn. It's time for me to stand aside and let them get on with it. I don't resent that, Peggy. A chapter is closed. A new one begins. The wheel turns. You see, when you get to my age, you accept that, Peggy. I'm not saying I didn't make my mark. I did. In my own way I revolutionized Warburtons. Incidentally that reminds me. I've got something I want you to take.

(MR DODSWORTH *goes out into the hall and can be heard rummaging under the stairs.*)

(*Off*) When I left I told Mr Skinner I'd let him have this, when I can find it. You can take it him, if you don't mind. Here we are.

(*He comes in with a large, flat parcel wrapped in worn brown paper and tied with string. He tears off the brown paper. It is very dusty.*)

Recognize this?

(*It is a framed chart of inter-office procedure, chains of authority, Central, District, Sub-District, and so on, drawn up in an elaborate and decorative way, in various colours. It may be more convenient to have it on a roll of paper, rather than in a frame.*)

MISS PROTHERO: I recognize it of course. It's the old revised lay-out.

51

MR DODSWORTH: It's basically the same as the one we have in the office
but old Mr Trowbridge in Design . . . except it wasn't called Design
then, in the Drawing Shop . . . I got him to make me a bit fancier one
for Winnie really. She used to hear me talking about the lay-out that
much, I had it done for her. It's a nice thing, I thought it'd go well in
Mr Skinner's office. Mind it's a bit mucky. I'll get a cloth. (*He goes
out.*)

MISS PROTHERO: Well! This brings back memories!
(*It may only be because the diagram is dirty but* MISS PROTHERO *is
looking at it with some disdain.* MR DODSWORTH *returns with a cloth and
cleans it up whereupon she condescends to look closer and even seems
interested.*)

MR DODSWORTH: It's only the names that are different . . . and there's the
three new departments but basically it's the same set-up as we've got
today. Fancy (*He points to the date.*) 1947! It was cold. Bitter cold.
We used to be starved stiff. Everybody in Credit and Settlement
used to be sat there in their overcoats.

MISS PROTHERO: I remember. The place must have been a shambles then.

MR DODSWORTH: It was, Peggy. It was.

MISS PROTHERO: No system at all.

MR DODSWORTH: How could there be a system when filing was on three
floors. You'd be running up and down those stairs all afternoon
looking for a voucher and then find it was over at Dickinson Road all
the time. It beats me how we ever got any payments in at all in them
days.

MISS PROTHERO: It was old Mr Warburton's fault. Nobody could do
anything with him stuck there.

MR DODSWORTH: If you've built a firm up from being one room then
naturally you think you know best.

MISS PROTHERO: He was the only one who knew where anything was.
You should delegate. He couldn't delegate.

MR DODSWORTH: By but he was a worker! There till ten every night.

MISS PROTHERO: But there was no system. System is what you want. It
was all hand to mouth.

MR DODSWORTH: I tell you, Peggy . . .
(*There is no need to tell Peggy anything. She is sitting there, smiling a
distant smile because she knows it all and a great deal more besides.*)
when I first took over in Credit and Settlement I did nothing at all
for about a month. I just sat there in that office in my overcoat trying
to fathom it all out. How it functioned. How it should function.
How it could be made to function. And eventually I thought, 'Well,

Arthur, if you can only get the filing on to a proper footing that'll be a start.' I reckoned that'd maybe take two or three months at the outside. Do you know how long it took? Four years. But I reckon that four years saved Warburtons thousands, hundreds of thousands in the end. Because out of it came ... (*He refers to all this on the diagram.*) direct debiting, inter-departmental docketing, direct directorial access, the marrying of receipts and invoices and really, all the lay-out of the new complex. It's all here. In embryo. Do you know what the turn round was when I first came into that office?

MISS PROTHERO: Ten days.

MR DODSWORTH: Three weeks. And you know what it was when I left? Well, you know what it was when I left. Forty-eight hours. And there it is. All I like to think is that when the fifth floor rings up for a 237 and it's there in five minutes there'll be somebody thinking—'Thank you, Arthur Dodsworth.'
Anyway, you take it. Give it Mr Skinner with my compliments. I'm not wanting to rush you off but you don't want to miss your bus. I'll put you some clean paper round it.
(MR DODSWORTH *rummages in a drawer.*)

MISS PROTHERO: The trouble is Mr Skinner's very particular about anything on the walls. He had Doreen take down all her postcards. And Mr Teasdale's silly notices. 'You don't have to be mad to work here but it helps.' I never thought that was funny. Mr Skinner didn't either. Now the walls are confined to relevant information.

MR DODSWORTH: This is relevant information, right enough. The basics are the same as they are today. I took him through it before I left. He soon had the hang of it. Of course that's the beauty of it. Logic and simplicity. (MR DODSWORTH *gets* MISS PROTHERO's *coat from the hall.*) Still if you don't want to take it, I'll pop by with it sometime.

MISS PROTHERO: I should hang on to it. It'll be like your clock. A memento.

MR DODSWORTH: Peggy. This is a working diagram.

MISS PROTHERO: Things have changed.

MR DODSWORTH: Not basically. Basically things are the same. (*He stops and looks at her.*) Aren't they?

MISS PROTHERO: That's what I've been trying to say. Only you would go on about all the things you were doing, wider worlds than Warburtons.

MR DODSWORTH: What things?

MISS PROTHERO: Cookery classes, pottery. Cordon Bleu.

MR DODSWORTH: What things?

MISS PROTHERO: I shall miss my bus.

53

MR DODSWORTH: You won't. That clock's fast.

MISS PROTHERO: Your presentation clock fast? You've not had it six months.

MR DODSWORTH: I didn't like to say. The electric's poor here. I think that affects it. You said things have changed. What things?

(MISS PROTHERO *sits down heavily.*)

MISS PROTHERO: Everything.

MR DODSWORTH: *Everything?*

MISS PROTHERO: You haven't really left me much time. However. When I think the damage was done was that first Monday.

(MISS PROTHERO *is determined to catch her bus. She is also determined to tell* MR DODSWORTH *everything. Speed is of the essence.*)

MR DODSWORTH: What first Monday?

MISS PROTHERO: Mr Skinner's . . . his first Monday we had a really shocking run of 476s and then to cap it all Costing sent up a couple of 248s . . . I mean, I think they were trying it on.

MR DODSWORTH: They would be. You don't get a 248 once in six months and two together, I never had that in thirty-odd years.

MISS PROTHERO: Well, that put him wrong side out for a start.

MR DODSWORTH: Why didn't he just docket them and get the whole lot carted off to the fifth floor?

MISS PROTHERO: What I said to Doreen Glazier. I think he just didn't want to go running upstairs on his first day. It's understandable, but anyway the upshot was we had to go through the whole rigmarole. Those two 248s took all day.

MR DODSWORTH: Costing, they want their backsides kicking.

MISS PROTHERO: The next thing I hear he's been in to see Mr Skidmore.

MR DODSWORTH: Mr Skidmore!

MISS PROTHERO: Mr Skidmore. He gives him the green light and do you know what the first thing he does is? Revamps the entire docketing system.

MR DODSWORTH: But there was nothing wrong with the docketing system.

MISS PROTHERO: Don't tell *me*. I thought of you, Mr Dodsworth. I thought, well I'm glad Mr Dodsworth isn't here to see this. I ran into Mr Butterfield in Accounts. He knew what was happening.

MR DODSWORTH: He would.

MISS PROTHERO: No, I said to him it would break Mr Dodsworth's heart. It would have broken your heart.

MR DODSWORTH: That's a funny way of going on. You can't mess about with docketing while you've got receipts and invoices married up.

MISS PROTHERO: Right. A fortnight later they were separated.

MR DODSWORTH: But it took me four years to get them together.

MISS PROTHERO: It took him two weeks to get them apart. After that it was a short step to Direct Departmental Debiting.

MR DODSWORTH: That would have to be entirely restructured.

MISS PROTHERO: Scrapped.

MR DODSWORTH: Scrapped!

MISS PROTHERO: We were knee deep in 5D forms and you know Maintenance are never there when they're wanted: I was actually taking them downstairs and bundling them into the incinerator myself. And of course who should I run into on one of the trips but Mr Sillitoe, who was with me my first year in C and S, do you remember, and he laughed and he said ...

MR DODSWORTH: But what's happened about filing?

MISS PROTHERO: Oh, did I not tell you that? I thought I'd told you that. Filing was all computerized in September anyway. You see what you have to remember about Mr Skinner is that he was six months at Newport Pagnell. He's got all that at his finger tips.

MR DODSWORTH: Well, I don't care what you say, our turn round was forty-eight hours. You can't get much slicker than that.

MISS PROTHERO: Halved.

MR DODSWORTH: Halved?

MISS PROTHERO: Halved.

MISS PROTHERO: Twenty-four hours now, and Mr Skinner says that's only a stage not a target. He envisages something in the range of twelve hours ... even, you'll laugh at this, even same day turnover.

MR DODSWORTH: You'll kill yourselves.

MISS PROTHERO: No. Half-past four and I'm generally just sat there. All done and docketed.

MR DODSWORTH: What about that ... inter-departmental docketing?

MISS PROTHERO: Oh we still do that.

MR DODSWORTH: That's something.

MISS PROTHERO: Only it's all in alphabetical order now.

MR DODSWORTH: Alphabetical order! What kind of a system is that!

MISS PROTHERO: Listen, I must go.

MR DODSWORTH: I don't see it. What happens ... what happens if you get a 318 and a 247 on the same sheet? If you don't have direct departmental debit you've got the whole process to go through on two separate dockets.

MISS PROTHERO: Can't happen. Not under the Skinner system. You see they couldn't be on the same sheet in the first place.

MR DODSWORTH: They could be on separate receipt dockets but on the same 348.

MISS PROTHERO: Yes, that happened on Friday. Mr Skinner fed it into the computer and it sorted it out in no time.

MR DODSWORTH: I think that's an admission of failure.

MISS PROTHERO: It only takes two minutes.

MR DODSWORTH: Computers, what are they? Glorified adding machines.

MISS PROTHERO: Don't let Mr Skinner hear you say that. He says a computer is an instrument of the imagination. He says that with another computer, me and Miss Glazier he could run Credit and Settlement single handed.

MR DODSWORTH: That's Newport Pagnell talking.

MISS PROTHERO: I didn't want to tell you all this but you would drag it out of me.

MR DODSWORTH: I just want to get a pencil and paper.

MISS PROTHERO: I must run.

MR DODSWORTH: Hang on a sec ... (*He starts making calculations.*)

MISS PROTHERO: It's a waste of time. You won't crack it. We've been going now for nearly four months and, as I say, Mr Skinner runs that office with the smoothness of a well-oiled machine.

MR DODSWORTH: You could catch the ten to, not the twenty past.

MISS PROTHERO: I've my supper to get.

MR DODSWORTH: You could have your supper here.

MISS PROTHERO: It's getting dark. Still I can call again. I thought you'd be lonely. I said to Doreen. I bet he's lonely. And it's made a nice little outing. You get out of touch.

MR DODSWORTH: It's true. I'd not realized.

MISS PROTHERO: Tell you what I can do. If I come again ...

MR DODSWORTH: No, you must come.

MISS PROTHERO: ... and that's fetch you some copies of the 114s. Glenda'll run me off one or two if I ask her nicely and then you'll be able to see how the procedure works, and that'll set your mind at rest.

MR DODSWORTH: Would you do that? That *is* good of you. Oh, Peggy, I should be ever so grateful ...

MISS PROTHERO: Well, we always had a soft spot for one another you and me, didn't we? Bye bye. (*She mouths this silently.*)

MR DODSWORTH: (*Following her into the hall*) And think on, call round any time. I shall be here. I won't go out. I'll make a point of not going out. Thank you ever so much for coming. Take care.

(*The front door closes. There is a pause and* MR DODSWORTH *comes slowly back into the room. He closes the door and picks up the chart, looks at it for a moment or two, then puts it down. He goes over to the birdcage, but without speaking to the bird.*

MR DODSWORTH *stands in his sitting-room feeling his whole life has been burgled, the contents of the years ransacked and strewn about the room. Some items he knows have gone and as the days pass he will remember others. Next time* MISS PROTHERO *will tell him more; and he will have less. He sits down in his chair.*)

MR DODSWORTH: Oh, Winnie, Winnie.